INTERRUPTING

THE

BIG SLEEP

JANICE MARRIOTT

illustrated by Don De Macedo

Learning Media

CHAPTER 1

At last it is morning.
I am cold. I am stiff.
My skin is dry and tight.
I want to peel it off.

I'm so bored.
Time is slowing down.

The wind hums through the creosote bushes.
I wait for a lick of sunlight.
I know the sun's path.
Soon it will come to this rock.
But, until it reaches me, I can't move.
Hurry up, sun!

At last! I feel the warmth on my back.
I stretch.
I open my jaws.
I stick out my tongue.

I slide off the rock and go to find breakfast.
But I don't forget that feeling of being helpless
when the frost is on the ground.

Now fall is suddenly here, and I have to find somewhere to hide for the winter.

Four whole months of freezing winter.

I hate the cold.

I have to keep warm.

I'll travel by day.
It's too cold at night.
At night, I'll sleep.
I know the way to go.
I've done it before. The canyon to the east,
the climb up the cliffs, the prickly pears.
It's time for a change.
I hide at the base of a cactus
where something has eaten out a hole.

Hidden from those hunting me, I pull, squeeze,
and stretch myself.
I rip myself away from my old skin.
I haul myself, exhausted, tender,
and brightly colored, out of my skin.
I have added another link to my tail!
I am venomous.
I am a rattlesnake.
A western diamondback rattlesnake.

I'm searching for one big meal
before my big winter sleep.

CHAPTER 2

At last it's morning.
The boy looks out the window
and sees a white glitter on the desert.
No wonder he's cold! It's a frost!
His skin is dry and tight.
He wants to peel it off.

He rubs his leg to get the blood flowing.
He's so stiff with cold
that he can hardly walk down the stairs.
There's a huge stove down in the kitchen.
His uncle is feeding logs into the stove.
"Hi," says the boy.
The uncle says nothing.

The boy is bored.
What's he going to do this vacation?
He has to stay here a month
while his mom takes her final exams back east.

His uncle points to the table.
They start breakfast.
"This fall weather. The tourists love it,"
says his uncle. "I'll be busy."
People used to come to see the saguaro cactus,
which is huge and old.
Now, very few people come.

The boy hears the wind humming
through the creosote bushes.
He waits for a lick of sunlight
through the window.
He eats his cereal in silence, waiting.
At last! He feels the warmth on his back.
He sticks out his tongue at the sun.

He slides off the chair and goes out to explore.

"Where you goin'?" calls his uncle.

"I might explore some," he says.

"Don't go out of sight of the house or sheds."

"Why not?"

"Snakes. They move around at this time of year."

"I'm not afraid."

"The deadliest snake is the diamondback.
It kills most people it bites," his uncle says
in his slowed-down Arizona drawl.

"Oh, yeah?" says the boy.

Later, the Internet is boring.
His computer games are boring.
He wants to be doing something real.

"What's in the barn?" he asks.
His uncle is sitting in a dusty chair.
"Straw. Oats. Winter feed and bedding
for the horses."
"What else?"
"Nothing that'd interest a young fella like you."
"You don't think?"
"I don't reckon."

He knows there are more interesting
things in that barn. When his mother
was persuading him to come here,
she told him that his uncle
had an old Cadillac in that barn.

That's what he's come southwest to see.
That's what he's going to see.
When his uncle isn't looking,
he reckons.

"Why's the door shut if it's just grain and stuff?"

"Snakes. This time of year I don't risk nothing."

The boy looks out the window at the huge,
red barn with the great door. He looks very hard
at the small door cut into the big door.
It doesn't look too hard to open.

The boy goes for a walk in the chill wind.
A burning pain shoots into his leg.
No! He doesn't dare look down.
He can hardly run.
Back in the kitchen, he collapses.
"Got a cholla cactus spine stuck in your leg,
city boy."

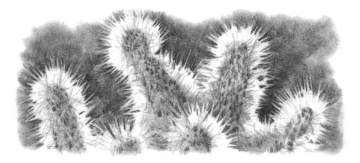

His uncle digs it out.
"Better watch where you're going."
The boy doesn't feel like going anywhere.

The feeling lasts only one hour.
Then he wants to explore that barn.
This new feeling doesn't go away.
He fights it for a whole week. Then he gives in.

CHAPTER 3

That chill wind makes me lazy.
I move slowly.
It's been a long journey,
but I'm nearly there.

I haul myself over a boulder
and around a prickly pear.
I'm almost at the hidden entrance
of my winter cave.

I'm very hungry.
Near my winter cave,
the desert seems to have emptied out.
I haven't heard an iguana,
a tortoise,
or those little birds in the cactus.

Last night, I couldn't even find a scorpion.
A tarantula squeezed under a stone,
but I couldn't reach it.
It wasn't very tempting, anyway.

I dream of eating peccary and pack rat.
One good, big pack rat would fill me up.
I'll open my huge jaws and slide over that rat.
Then I'll swallow.
The great swelling will stay there inside me
for maybe two weeks, while my juices
slowly attack it.
They'll dissolve it, bit by bit,
while I sleep The Big Sleep and dream.

And dream.

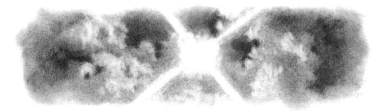

I will dream of a round, red sun.

But I can't find anything to eat.
The world around me is bright blue and red
and orange, in lumps and blotches.
It's the hot colors, the reds and oranges,
that interest me – they're the living things,
the hot-blooded things that I'm looking for.

Have I left it too late to sleep?
I hope not.
I'm here now, near my secret cave.
I'll be with piles of other sleeping diamondbacks.
But before I slide under that rock outcrop,
I have to eat!

I wait, out in the open.
It's quiet.
Through my belly,
I can feel if the ground moves,
even the tiniest movement of a lizard or a bird.

I am a great hunter.

Who needs hands? I don't.

Suddenly there's a movement!
Moving air above me! No!
That means danger.
I can't see it coming, but I know it's there.
I can't see its shadow rushing across
the canyon sides.
I fear those cruel, curved talons.
It's coming! A red-tailed hawk!

It dives at me out of the sun.
I feel that rush of air across my back.

I slither as fast as I can under the rock overhang, through a dry streambed.
I squeeze between two rocks.
I am at the secret entrance to my winter cave.

The hawk can't get me here.
I'm safe.

I use my rattle as a warning. Keep away!
But in front of me are boulders,
rubble, dried mud.
The entrance to the winter cave is blocked!

I have to find somewhere else.

CHAPTER 4

The boy opens the door of the barn
and peers in.
The barn is warm and sweet-smelling.
There are no horses now, but it's full of old hay.
In the middle of the floor is a black car.
It's the Cadillac!

It's huge, with thick, chrome bumpers.
He walks up to it and brushes the dust away.
It's like peeling off a fur coat.
He sees the gleaming paint.

This is what he's been looking for.
It's like finding treasure.
He loves cars.

He never ever sees old cars back east.
Hardly anyone has a garage in Newark.
They'd have nowhere to put one.

But out here, where the land is vast and empty,
people spread out with big hats, big houses,
big cars, and vast barns.

The car is a four-door sedan. He thinks
it'd be 1950s. He's seen this kind in books.

He likes the small triangle windows.
He rubs his hand along the fat back bumper
and then around the sharp taillights on the fins.
Fins! Cars don't have fins now.
He wishes they did.

Quietly, he walks round the chunky car.
There's a strip of chrome all along the side.
When he's at the front again, he stands on
the bumper and stretches across the long hood.
A rustle! What was that?
He waits, still as a stone.
The rustle came from a bale of hay.
He tiptoes over to it and sees the skinny,
long slither of a rat's tail disappearing under some
old oil drums.

His heart's hammering.
His uncle's snake story has freaked him.
Stupid Uncle. A rat isn't going to scare him.
He walks back to the car and tries
the driver's door.
It's unlocked.
In front of him is one long seat.
He slides onto
the smooth gray leather.
There's a woman's scarf on the seat.
He throws it into the back.

He moves the gearshift and runs his hand along
the sloping dashboard.
It juts out like a rock overhang.

He holds the wheel.
In the middle, there's a big, round, silver hub.
He stares at it.
It's like an eye, staring back at him.
A magic eye.

He looks down at the huge speedometer.
He slowly stretches his right arm
but he can't touch the passenger door.
He winds his window down.
Then he rests his left arm on the armrest
in the door, and he dreams.
And dreams.
He dreams he's being swallowed up
by this huge car.
His heart has slowed right down.

"Jack!" calls his uncle from the house porch.
"Where are you? Your mother's on the phone.
They're having floods back east."

"So what," the boy thinks, still slowed down.
"We're ten floors up in our block.
Nothing to worry about."
But he has to go.
Will his uncle see him slip out the barn door?

It'll be nice to hear his mother's voice, he thinks,
sliding away from the car without a sound.

He doesn't shut the car door because he doesn't want to break the magic silence.

His uncle's standing right outside the barn door. They say nothing to each other.

Without realizing it, he's left the door of the barn slightly open too.

After talking to his mom,
he finds his uncle oiling a cracked old saddle
out by the rusty gates of the ranch.
The boy can tell that the saddle is useless.

There are two stone pillars,
a saguaro cactus,
and a billboard with a saguaro painted on it.
"There isn't much of a welcome here,"
thinks the boy. "And hardly any tourists
stop by."

He tells his uncle he's bored and cold and has
nothing to do.

"I play on the Internet, but I want something real to happen."
His uncle says nothing.
"Take me for a drive in the old Cadillac?"
he asks.
"No!" his uncle says.
"Let me sit in it, then."
"No!"
"Let me look at it."
"No!"
His uncle is mean.

Then his uncle says that when he was young and had a wife and kids,
he used to take the car out for
the occasional Sunday drive.
He loved the feel of the gears, the big pedals,
the mirrors. "But no more. They've gone.
And it don't seem much point,
driving around in a huge hulk like that
by myself now, does it?"

There is silence between them.

The uncle keeps polishing round and round
on the saddle.
The boy watches the white circles on
the brown leather.
He doesn't move.

The uncle sighs, puts down his cloth,
and looks out at the old barn.
"She was a good-looker, that woman.
She sat there beside me, and it was a sight.
Folks'd stare as we drove past."

The boy whispers, "You could drive me.
Then it wouldn't be just yourself."

The uncle stares at him a long time
from heavy-lidded eyes.
It's like he's gone to sleep.
Then he grabs his cloth
and continues rubbing the saddle.
"Nah! Wouldn't be the same thing, little 'un."

The boy goes into the house.
His uncle has forgotten to tell him off
for going into the barn.

He gets a drink and watches big ants
trembling after each other
along the kitchen bench.

Then he decides to go back to the barn.

CHAPTER 5

It's still daylight.
I'm near humans.
I'm in danger,
but it's too cold to travel at night.
I have to find a warm place to sleep
the winter through.

I'm slithering along a dry ditch.
I come to two stone pillars
and a huge saguaro cactus
with tiny birds hopping about it.

I'm dreaming about a rabbit,
but a bird would be better than nothing.
I wrap myself into a puddle of shade
at the base of the old cactus and wait.

My tongue flicks out.
I taste the air to find a bird.
I can tell that something warm is near.

I wait for a bird to flutter to the ground.

Through my belly, I feel one land very close.
I rear up two feet high in the air.
I strike.
I pour venom through my fangs.
Then I wait until it's all over for the bird.

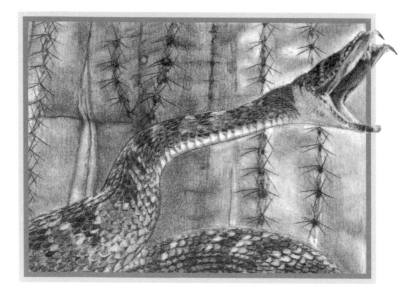

I swallow it whole.
A small meal, but I'm not complaining.

I slide, wriggle, and glide from bush to stone
to ditch, looking, always looking.

Then I see it. A dark place, with warmth inside.
A small opening.
I slither in.

This cave is warm and sweet-smelling.
It's full of dried grass and shadowy corners.
But I smell humans.

If I stay here, I will need to hide very well.
In the middle of the floor is a dark shape.
In it, there's an opening, smooth and warm.
It will have to do.
A safe place for the winter.
It's like finding treasure.

There are no other diamondbacks in here.
I glide down, under, deep into darkness
and a corner.
I am so tired.

Then I feel heat.
Heat! Some other living thing is here too.

I flick out my tongue.
OK. I know what it is, but I ignore it
for the moment.
It's a tarantula. The biggest I've known.
There are bound to be lots of them
in places like this.

CHAPTER

6

The uncle stands by the peeling
and cracked welcome sign,
wondering how he can repaint it.
His wife was the painter, not him.

The boy sneaks back into the barn.
He creeps up to the car and squeezes
quietly onto the front seat.

He turns the steering wheel.
He dreams.

Suddenly he hears a scratching, pricking noise.
Something is moving behind his neck!
He sees movement out of the corner of his eye.
He dares not turn round.

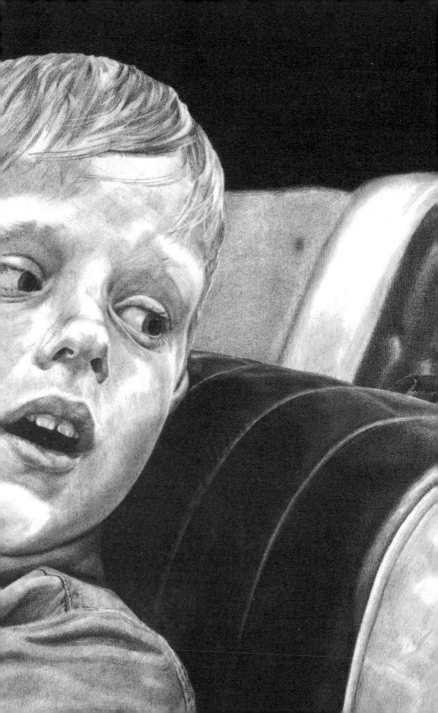

"Don't be a coward," he says to himself.
"It's probably another rat."

The movement and the pricking sound
don't feel like a rat.
They feel slower, more delicate, and very scary.

He rolls his eyes up, slowly.
"Don't move a muscle," he thinks.
Up. Up. His eyes roll until he can look
in the rearview mirror.
There's something there behind him,
something dark.
A round shape is rising up onto the top
of the seat from behind.

First, two waving hairy legs,
and then a head, of sorts.
After the head comes a huge,
round lump of a body. It shivers.

The tarantula is as big as the boy's palm.

It is now perched on top of the back of his seat,
about six inches from his neck.
It rears up suddenly.
The two front legs grab at the air
beside the boy's ear.

Then the giant spider settles
among its legs on the top corner of the seat,
beside the driver's door.

The boy is trapped.

Time stands still.

The boy's eyes slide away to the silver hub
at the middle of the Cadillac's wheel.
He feels stronger, braver.

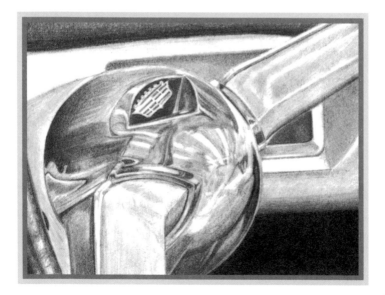

He is not going to be scared of a spider.
Slowly, he stretches out his arm and leans
across the long front seat.
His arm seems to grow, like a snake.
Stretch! Stretch! Nearly – there!
He pushes down on the door handle.
The spider hasn't moved.

Suddenly he flings himself across the seat
and out of the car.

His heart is revving in high gear.

He picks himself up and slams the door shut.
He gulps in air.
He feels sick.
When the huge noise of the door slam
stops echoing through the dark barn,
he hears a sound unlike anything
he's ever heard before.

It's a buzzing, a sizzling, a rattling sound.
It's a sound that ices up his insides.

Through the cracked window
of the car's back seat,
he sees a massive brown and black and white
snake rise from a coil and strike at the inside of
the window.
He notices its forked flicking tongue,
the stripe from its head down to its lidless eye.

Then he runs.

He calls to his uncle.
"Help! Help me!"

And his uncle wakes up, out of a great slowness
he's been in since his wife left.

He rushes to his nephew.
He hugs him.
They cling together.
Then, together, and for the rest of the day,
they excitedly plan what to do.

What to do with the snake and the spider.
What to do with the Cadillac.
And what to do with everything
in their suddenly fast-moving lives.